MW00887737

Fiddleheads to Fir Trees

LEAVES IN ALL SEASONS

Joanne Linden

ILLUSTRATED BY
Laurie Caple

2013
MOUNTAIN PRESS PUBLISHING COMPANY
MISSOULA, MONTANA

For my children and grandchildren:
Katie, Jane, Mike, Emilie, and Jack
—J. L.

For Guy and Linda ❤
—L. C.

ACKNOWLEDGMENTS

With special thanks to my critique groups; my editor,
Jenn Carey; and my illustrator, Laurie Caple.

The illustrator would like to thank the staff members at Hunt Hill Audubon
Sanctuary and the Minnesota Landscape Arboretum for their assistance in
locating and identifying leaf specimens. A special thanks to André van Jaarsveld.

Text © 2013 by Joanne Linden
Illustrations © 2013 by Laurie Caple

First Printing, August 2013

Library of Congress Cataloging-in-Publication Data

Linden, Joanne.
Fiddleheads to fir trees : leaves in all seasons / Joanne Linden ; illustrated by Laurie Caple.
    pages cm
ISBN 978-0-87842-606-5 (alk. paper)
1. Leaves—Juvenile literature. I. Caple, Laurie A., illustrator. II. Title.
QK649.L56 2013
575.5'7—dc23

2013013219

PRINTED IN HONG KONG BY MANTEC PRODUCTION COMPANY

 Mountain Press
PUBLISHING COMPANY
P.O. Box 2399 • Missoula, MT 59806 • 406-728-1900
800-234-5308 • info@mtnpress.com
www.mountain-press.com

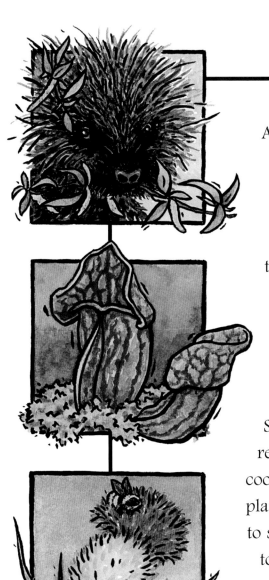

All around the world plants are growing—
in woods, swamps, fields, and meadows.
In springtime, leaves emerge from buds
or poke up from the ground. The leaves
unfold into perfect green shapes, ready
to begin their important work. Leaves use
energy from the sun to make food for
the plants. The energy helps the plants
grow and produce flowers and seeds.

As spring rolls into summer, insects
and animals munch on the leaves.
Sometimes plants will make new leaves to
replace the old, damaged ones. Fall brings
cooler temperatures and shorter days. As the
plants get ready for winter, most leaves turn
to shades of brown, red, and yellow and fall
to the ground.

Let's take a journey through the seasons
to see some remarkable leaves of different
shapes, sizes, and colors. Some are large and
round, and others are thin and
narrow. Some are fuzzy with little
hairs, and others are smooth as glass.
The leaves of the pitcher plant can
even trap insects. Come, I'll show you.

Fiddleheads

Fuzzy rust overcoats burst.
Tight green coils like carved scrolls on a violin
Strain . . . stretch . . . spiral
Upward.

Wisp by wisp
Feathery leaves
Uncurl
And reach for the light.

FEATHERY LEAVES

Baby ferns, called fiddleheads, look like the curled part at the top of a stringed instrument, such as a violin or fiddle. When they first appear, growing close to the ground, they are about the length of your big toe. You can find them in early spring, basking in bright sunlight before the trees leaf out and shade them. Rabbits, chipmunks, and squirrels nibble on these tender shoots. As the weather gets warmer, the stems and leaves uncurl into feathery ferns.

Curly-leaf Pondweed

Curly leaves
sway in rippled water,

Twisting

    Twirling

        Tickling

the swimmers' legs
like snakes slithering
along a log.

WEEDY LEAVES

Curly-leaf pondweed gets its name from the wavy edges of its leaves. These dark green to reddish plants are weedy. They form thick mats in the shallow water of ponds and lakes. Sometimes they clog waterways, making it difficult to boat or swim. They are one of the first underwater plants to grow in the spring. In fact, they can even start to grow beneath the ice in late winter. Young fish hide among the waving leaves.

DROOPING LEAVES

The weeping willow gets its name from its sweeping branches that droop almost to the ground. They appear to be bowed down with sadness. These graceful trees like moist soil and often grow along lakes or streams. The long, narrow leaves have olive green tops and silvery bottoms that shimmer in the sunlight. In spring, porcupines and other animals eat the young leaves and fuzzy flowers, called catkins.

Weeping Willow

Graceful branches

Arch
       over the rocky shore,
Bend
       drooping arms, and
Reach
       slender fingertips,

Down to the glassy stream,

To touch reflections reaching up.

Water Lilies

Flat, shiny circles
float on quiet water.

A fat basking croaker

lifts off
    from his drifting launch pad
      and falls . . .
           Kerplunk!

Wet bobbing lily pad.

FLOATING LEAVES

Water lilies grow in shallow water near the edges of lakes and ponds. Their large, circular leaves, called lily pads, float on the water's surface. They are attached to flexible stalks that rise from the muddy bottom. The wide, flat surface of each leaf, which can be almost a foot across, soaks up the sunshine. Frogs rest on these green platforms, waiting for bugs to fly by, but hop away when danger nears. Beavers and muskrats feed on the rubbery lily pads and roots.

HUNGRY LEAVES

The leaves of the pitcher plant form a long tube that looks like a vase or a water pitcher. Inside the tube are tiny hairs that point downward and create a slippery, waxy surface. Insects, which are attracted by the plant's fragrant smell, enter the tube and cannot get out. They slip down the greasy slide into the watery pool below and drown.

The plant uses nutrients from the dead bugs to grow.

Pitcher Plant

Cupped leaves like green china
catch early morning rain
to make a pitfall trap.

An unsuspecting fly tumbles,

    Slips . . .

        Slides . . .

        Down the pitcher's waxy throat.

Breakfast is served.

Catalpa

A canopy of hearts
    curves overhead.
A secret place to sit
    quiet and alone.
Green seedpods
    like slender beans
Dangle from the branches
And click~clack in the breeze.
A shady summer retreat.

HEART-SHAPED LEAVES

The large leaves of the catalpa tree provide a shady canopy, protecting birds and other animals from the sun and rain. The heart-shaped leaves embrace long beans that hang down from the branches. These hard-shelled beans can grow to be ten to sixteen inches long. When they dry and turn brown in the fall, they make a click-clack sound as they bump each other in the wind.

Thistle

Lavender beauty,
Your flowers burst forth
With purple crowns that nod hello.
But your prickles keep us away from you.
Can't you make up your mind?
Will you be friendly?
Or not?

PRICKLY LEAVES

The leaves of
thistles have
prickly spines
on their tips and
edges. These stiff
spines hurt when
you touch them and
can puncture your skin.
While the prickles keep
animals from eating the
plant, the thistle's beautiful
lavender flowers attract
butterflies with their nectar.
Seed-loving birds, such as
goldfinches and pine siskins, eat
thistle seeds while perching
carefully among the spines.

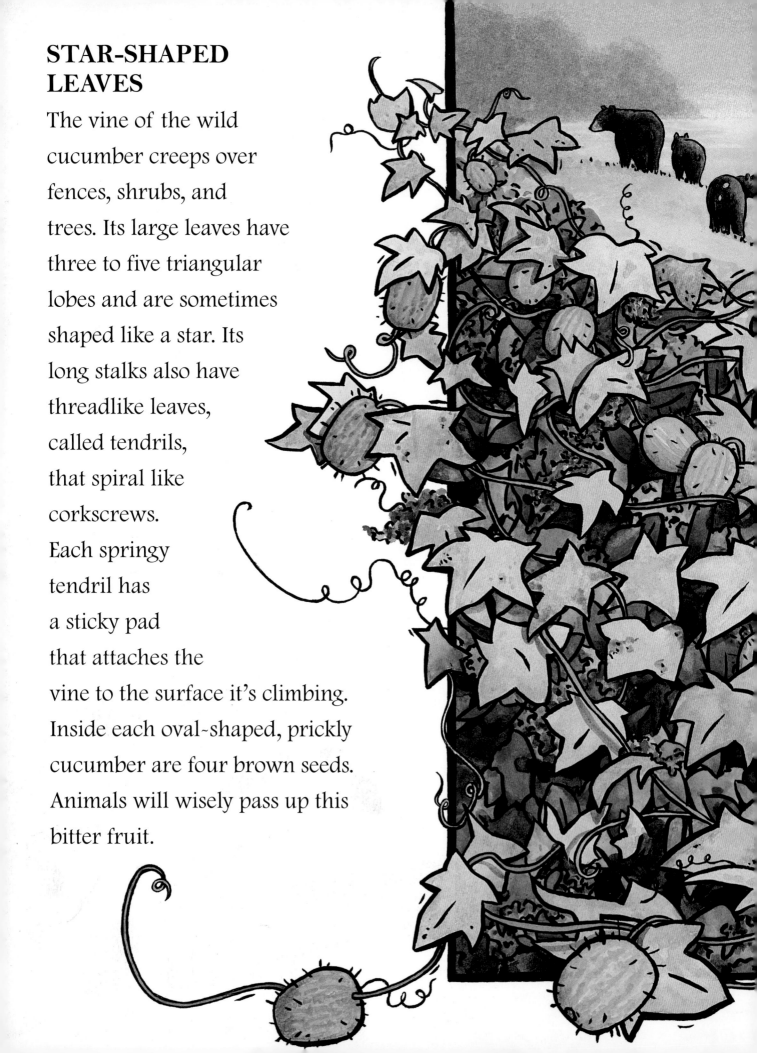

STAR-SHAPED LEAVES

The vine of the wild cucumber creeps over fences, shrubs, and trees. Its large leaves have three to five triangular lobes and are sometimes shaped like a star. Its long stalks also have threadlike leaves, called tendrils, that spiral like corkscrews. Each springy tendril has a sticky pad that attaches the vine to the surface it's climbing. Inside each oval-shaped, prickly cucumber are four brown seeds. Animals will wisely pass up this bitter fruit.

Wild Cucumber

Star-pointed lobes drape in long scarves over meadow bushes.

Light green
cucumbers hang
from twisted vines.
Prickly oval pouches
hold black seeds
ready to drop.

Milkweed

M auve milkweeds hold
I nching caterpillars.
L eaves, oozing milky sap,
K eep monarchs safe from
W atchful birds.
E ach brown seedpod bursts.
E scaping silky fluffs
D epart for distant meadows.

SPRING

SUMMER

MILKY LEAVES

The fuzzy leaves of milkweed contain a poisonous milky sap. The caterpillar of the monarch butterfly can feed on the leaves without being harmed. When the caterpillar finishes eating, it spins a cocoon. In two weeks or less, a beautiful monarch butterfly is born. The monarch contains the milkweed poison in its body, so birds will not eat it. Milkweed forms crescent-shaped seed-pods that turn brown in the fall and crack open. They release seeds with fluffs of silk that float in the air.

Quaking Aspen

Flutter, Shiver
Shake and Quiver
   Rustle, rustle, swish
Trembling leaves
Timid leaves
   Whisper gibberish.

TREMBLING LEAVES

The leaves of the quaking aspen flutter in the slightest breeze. The name *quaking* refers to this trembling motion. As leaves brush against each other, they create a pleasant swishing sound, a peaceful tune for an afternoon nap. This fast-growing tree loves the sun, and scientists think the fluttering motion allows leaves to get more sunlight. It may also discourage bugs. The leaves of quaking aspen, like those of other deciduous trees, change color in autumn when the days get shorter and there is less sunshine.

Poison Ivy

Leaflets three
on sturdy stems
bow to the morning sun.
Colored faces honor
crisp September skies.
Bold orange and crimson red,
autumn jewels linger,
as oily resins hitch a ride
with unsuspecting hikers brushing by.
Sneaky leaves!

SPRING

SUMMER

SNEAKY LEAVES

Poison ivy grows in fields, along streams, at the edges of woods, and in ditches along roads. It can look like a ground cover, a climbing vine, or a bush, making it tricky to identify. Its leaves, which come in groups of three, are red in spring, green in summer, and yellow, red, and orange in fall. These harmless-looking leaves transfer an oily residue onto anyone or anything that brushes up against them. The oil causes a red, itchy rash on the skin of the unsuspecting victim. Heed the warning: Leaves of three; let it be.

SCALY LEAVES

The evergreen leaves of cedar are flat and scaly. They contain a fragrant oil that is rich in vitamin C. Native Americans and early explorers drank tea made from cedar leaves to prevent scurvy, a disease caused by the lack of vitamin C. Jacques Cartier, a French explorer, gave this tree the common name of *arborvitae*, which means "tree of life." It gives life to hungry critters in winter when little else is available to eat. White-tailed deer, moose, snowshoe hares, and other animals munch heavily on cedar leaves.

Cedar

Scale
    by
        scale
            by
                scale
Evergreen shingles overlap
Thin woody twigs.
Leathery layers coat
Flat fragrant sprays,
            scale
          by
            scale
       by
scale.
The scent escapes
on the wind.

BLADED LEAVES

Cattails are in the grass family. Their narrow leaves resemble giant blades of grass and can grow longer than a person is tall. Native Americans wove these long leaves into sturdy mats. Cattails, which grow in wet areas, have fuzzy brown flower spikes. If you pull them apart, hundreds of very small seeds attached to fluff will blow away in the wind. The long leaves and brown spikes last long into winter, providing shelter and hiding places for white-tailed deer and other animals.

Cattails

Long sturdy blades
Rise up,
Spears aimed at the sun.

Brown velvet spikes
Salute
The new day.

Brave soldiers
Stand alert.
Guardians of the marsh.

FRAGRANT LEAVES

The leaves of balsam fir
are flat needles that stay
on the tree year-round. The
densely packed needles
and branches of this
evergreen tree provide
winter shelter for
animals. The cones point
skyward, unlike those
of spruce trees, which
hang down. The balsam
fir is prized as a Christmas
tree because of its shape
and spicy scent. The smell
is from resin, a sticky,
oily liquid contained in
the needles and stems.
Glittering snow and
ice and colorful birds
decorate this festive
tree in
winter.

Balsam Fir

In
one
breath,
memory
awakens the
twinkling lights,
glittering ornaments,
and brightly wrapped packages.
An elegant princess is clad in her
holiday
garb.

CAN YOU FIND THESE ANIMALS IN THE BOOK?
(Look on the page with the plant noted.)

MAMMALS
Black Bear (Wild Cucumber, cover)

White-tailed Deer (Cedar, cover)

Red Fox (Balsam Fir, cover)

Porcupine (Weeping Willow, introduction page)

Eastern Cottontail Rabbit (Fiddleheads)

Red Squirrel (Poison Ivy, cover)

Gray Wolf (Cattails)

INSECTS
Bumblebee (introduction page)

Ladybird Beetle (title page)

Monarch Butterfly (Milkweed, cover)

Blue Darner Dragonfly (Water Lilies)

Dragonfly Skimmer (Pitcher Plant)

BIRDS
Northern Cardinal (Balsam Fir)

American Goldfinch (Thistle)

Great Blue Heron (Pitcher Plant)

Blue Jay (Catalpa, Balsam Fir, copyright page, cover)

Saw-whet Owl (Aspen)

REPTILES AND AMPHIBIANS
Green Frog (Water Lilies, cover)

Gray Tree Frog (Fiddleheads, cover)

Painted Turtle (Curly-leaf Pondweed, cover)

FISH
Fathead Minnow (Curly-leaf Pondweed)

ABOUT THE AUTHOR
Joanne Linden is a former elementary school teacher who writes poetry, stories, and nonfiction for children from her home in Wisconsin. She grew up in northern Minnesota near the Boundary Waters Canoe Area, where the boreal forest inspired her interest in natural history. When she's not reading, writing, and painting, she loves to spend time at her lake cottage with her husband and Auggie, their Scottish terrier. Joanne enjoys visits with her children and grandchildren.

ABOUT THE ILLUSTRATOR
Exploring forests and wading through ponds as a child in search of turtles and frogs set the stage for **Laurie Caple's** career as a children's book illustrator and natural history artist. A graduate of Michigan Technological University, Laurie has created artwork for numerous picture books and periodicals, such as *American Girl* and *Cricket*. Her primary medium is watercolor. Laurie lives in northern Wisconsin with her husband, two sons, two golden retrievers, and three turtles named Skittles, Snickers, and Sassafras.